CHOOSE YOUR OWN ADVENTURE®

SPIES:
MATA HARI

BY KATHERINE FACTOR

ILLUSTRATED BY CHLOE NICLAS

CHOOSECO
WAITSFIELD, VERMONT

Illustrated by: Chloe Niclas
Book design: Stacey Boyd, Big Eyedea Visual Design

For information regarding permission, write to:

CHOOSECO
P.O. Box 46
Waitsfield, Vermont 05673
www.cyoa.com

Published simultaneously in the United States and Canada

Printed in Canada

10 9 8 7 6 5 4 3 2 1

*For my sister, Abigail, and all
my dancing friends.*

BEWARE and WARNING!

This book is different from other books. YOU and you alone are in charge of what happens in this story.

Your stage name is Mata Hari, and you are a star dancer. You have toured the world performing for crowds who love your dances, and you meet important people and learn to speak their languages as you travel.

In 1915, you are on the island of Bali. Europe is divided by the first World War and your skills and connections make YOU a candidate to spy, for France or for Germany. Which side will you help? When you read this book, you will learn real things about what life was like in 1915. You will also make choices that determine YOUR own fate in the story. Choose carefully, because the wrong choice could end in disaster—even death. But don't despair. At any time, YOU can go back and make another choice, and alter the path of your fate…and maybe even history.

You peer out at the crowd from behind the curtains of the rustic theater where tonight's performance will take place.

Your name is Margaretha Zelle, and you are a world-famous dancer from the Netherlands. Your dance company arrived late last night to Bali. It's part of Indonesia; an island filled with Hindu temples, beaches, jungles, strange music, and magic.

Your dance troupe quivers beside you with excitement and nerves. Dame Moma, the troupe leader, is vigorously arranging and giving final orders to the newest dancers backstage. Your friends Scarlet, Anna, Ruth, Cleo, and Bella line up, stretching and running through their breathing exercises with anticipation.

It took your troupe a week to reach Bali by steamship from Thailand. It is 1915, and it is not common for young women to adventure alone, so you stay together and follow the rules.

Everyone in your troupe comes from different countries in Europe, where World War I is raging. Most people are not dancing or traveling with ease. You are very fortunate to be on tour.

Tonight is the biggest audition of your life! In the crowd are scouts for the Opera at La Scala in Milan, Italy. If you do well, they will select you for the Princess Dance, and you will perform in front of the largest, most influential crowds of your career.

Turn to the next page.

2

"This is your night, *Mata Hari!*" Dame Moma says to you in a hushed, insistent whisper. You are already famous all over the world under your artistic name, but you agree with the Dame. This is a night that could change your whole career.

It is show time! You adjust your maroon silk costume, embroidered with pearls. You pin your hair up in a snake-shaped crown. Your first dance is a dance in praise of the Balinese rice goddess. The live Gamelan band could not perform as promised due to a holiday, but there is a recording, which is what you are used to practicing with anyway.

When the lights go up, you think, *the Dame is right.* This moment is your destiny, what you've been training for all this time. First up, the ballerinas do classic work. Then, there is a number from Stravinsky, the new controversial composer. The crowd applauds wildly when you step on to the stage.

Go on to the next page.

You *glissando* out onstage with veils flapping like colored wind. There are importantly dressed people in the front rows—you know they are enchanted by your talent. You dance well, but not perfectly. Something feels wrong. At the intermission you realize what it is: Althea, the youngest of your troupe and your sweetest friend, is missing. You alert Dame Moma immediately, and you see she has already noticed, which makes you angry.

"Stop the performance!" you shout, thinking of young Althea alone in this very wild place, lost or worse, kidnapped.

"Listen to me, Margaretha. We must not panic," says Dame Moma forcefully. "The police have been alerted and are on their way. It will endanger all of us if you rush out into the jungle by yourself." She looks out at the empty stage for a moment, the crowd waiting for the dancers to return for the second half. "We are performers, and we must still do our job."

"You can't mean we will still perform without Althea?" you gasp.

Turn to the next page.

Dame Moma gives you a very stern look. "There are many foreign visitors here in Bali for the first time tonight, and we cannot cause alarm. You must continue the performance and show no fear on your face!"

You do as the Dame says and smile for the crowd when you return to the stage. But when you close your eyes mid-dance, you see your friend crying somewhere. You cannot help but think, *I must find her.*

When the troupe comes onstage to finish the piece, you realize this is your moment to do something to help Althea. Everyone is distracted and you can dance offstage and dash toward the exit. You stop for just a moment. If you leave, you will lose your chance at becoming a star.

If you dance offstage and escape to find Althea, turn to page 7.

If you stay and keep performing, turn to page 19.

Next, you learn basic survival skills. Your test is a night of camping, solo. You are terrified. Elsbeth and Mr. Astruc teach you how to make smoke signals and swear they will be nearby enough to see them. You sleep alone, hearing scary jungle sounds. You cry, feeling unglamorous.

"You survived! This is just the beginning," Elsbeth says when she retrieves you from the camp. "Since you are so young and starry-eyed, no one will suspect you. You are already physically strong and can withstand any trial!"

You believe her, even though you are overwhelmed with all the new challenges.

"Phew! I thought I was never getting out of there!" you say, relieved, when you return to your regular bed in Bali. You are exhausted but exhilarated. You begin Phase 2 of boot camp, which is the espionage, communications, and mental preparation, like how to hold a poker face and keep a secret.

You learn how to handle important documents, how to create poisons, create coded messages, and forge signatures. You learn how to slowly wave a fan to transmit a message, the art of eavesdropping, as well as how to secretly apply serums and poisons on forks and drinking glasses. You master all sorts of tools and contraptions: scarves that can be used to send coded messages, and your favorite: invisible ink.

"When can I use this ink? I really like my handwriting."

"Very soon. If you choose to chase the Dame."

Turn to page 26.

You hear the music queue for you to exit the stage. The other dancers enter to create the "living garden" part of the piece. Now is your chance! You leave the stage as if nothing is wrong, then dash past the distracted stage manager to the backstage door.

Quickly, you pull a veil from your costume, knotting it around the doorknob. Using all your muscle, you yank the scarf and break the lock. You dart like a thief outside onto the cobblestone street just as the music changes.

It is dark. You must not get caught and so keep moving. But where to start? You hear music in the distance and head in that direction. Perhaps Althea did the same! You run off in your costume and dance slippers, rough stone under your feet. You're panting when, *BLAM!* you stumble into something. "OUF! That stings!" you moan, stopping dead in your tracks. You look up and see a peculiar, robust man with a white beard.

Turn to the next page.

8

"Whoa there. Sorry about that," the man says, pulling out an exquisite gold chain with a blunt-edged round object attached. It is unusual, and definitely not a pocket watch.

"Ouch!" You rub your forehead where you smashed against the talisman. "That really smarts."

He spins the chain and it somehow switches on a flashlight. He shines it on your forehead. "You'll have a bruise there." As his fingertips touch the spot, the throbbing stops. He continues, "But, I can tell that inside of you something is *actually* wrong. Do tell me, for I am Monty-the-Magnificent! I can help you, you know."

Turn to page 10.

"Can you help me find my friend Althea?" you blurt out, and then explain the situation.

"Oh my, that is quite frightening. But…trust me, I know just what to do," says Monty. "Stand here, beside the white wall of this café," Monty tells you. He lifts up the talisman again and switches a gear to show you what appears to be a projection, aiming it at the café's wall like it's a cinema screen. You see Althea in a dark purple room. The air is waving like water. You can't tell if she is comfortable, or about to drown.

"Wow. How did you do that? Is that timepiece… magical?"

"I am a magician and spymaster; this is the only one of its kind," he states. "This all-seeing monocle I created will help us find her." Monty holds up the piece to his eye. It shines, blinding you.

You know there are explanations for most illusions from your time onstage, and you might not have time to waste on simple tricks. Maybe the music you heard was a better clue than this stranger and his fortune-telling watch.

If you follow the music in hopes of finding your friend, turn to page 34.

If you stick with the man who has some magic, turn to page 113.

You unfurl the scroll and smooth it out on the dock to examine it carefully. It has a fancy foil edge with embossed lettering.

Headley Grange
East Hampshire, England

You wonder how important that is to the mission. Then you see a chart below it.

To view it, turn to the next page.

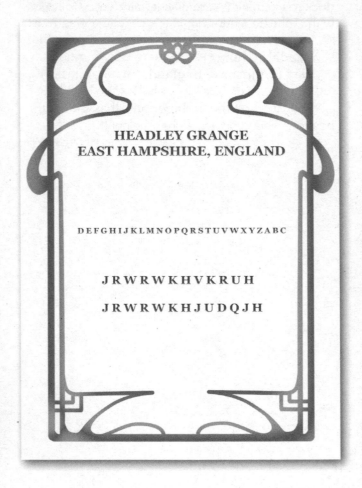

**HEADLEY GRANGE
EAST HAMPSHIRE, ENGLAND**

DEFGHIJKLMNOPQRSTUVWXYZABC

JRWRWKHVKRUH

JRWRWKHJUDQJH

Hmmm, you wonder as you examine it. It's the alphabet, but why does it start at "D?" You think back to your training and realize this must be a decoder key, used to explain a message that is written in a cipher somewhere else. Turning the music box three times made it work. Clockwise turns, to the right. Maybe this is how the key works?

You write out the full alphabet below the "key."

D E F G H I J K L M N O P Q R S T U V W X Y Z A B C

A B C D E F G H I J K L M N O P Q R S T U V W X Y Z

Turn to the next page.

14

"D" is three shifts down and it took three cranks to reveal the scroll. You think you have figured it out!!

DEFGHIJKLMNOPQRSTUVWXYZABC

ABCDEFGHIJKLMNOPQRSTUVWXYZ

You study and use the decoder. You take the first line of jumbled letters and begin to try to crack the code. You find "J" in the key and see that it matches to "G". Find each letter in the code and, using the real alphabet, fill in the rest of blanks below!

J	R	W	R	W	K	H	V	K	R	U	H
		T						H			

Turn to page 77.

You avoid the chaos by jaunting off, out of the public parade and into the jungle. Stumbling into flora, you charge through brush until you find a teeny dirt path. You are out of breath. You hold on to a bamboo tree.

Calm down. I will figure it out and find my friends, you insist to yourself.

You trek down the path but only feel more lost. It is really dark. It smells of calming sandalwood and flowers galore, but your nerves override the pleasant scents. You are on high alert. You hear a loud, mighty sound.

Turn to the next page.

16

"Who's there?!" you yell, certain the sound is a person approaching. You look toward the sound. Even though it is so dark, you *see* something shimmering in the near distance. You move through the swampy brush, and you find a glowing statue of a man with an ornate snake wrapped around him. Three arms—*three!*—spread out as if treading water. One palm is raised up facing you. The left foot is twisted up, crossed over the bent right leg. His hair resembles flaming wings spreading out.

You stare at the statue. *Why, it looks like it is dancing!*

Turn to page 18.

18

You wonder what dance it is, when suddenly, you are blinded by a flash of light. Then, the statue starts to wiggle and morph. It is coming alive! You can't believe your eyes as flames erupt in a circle around the clearing, flashing fire as the statue transforms into a deity before you.

"Whoa. Who are you? What are you?"

"I am Shiva, Lord of the Dance!"

"Oh wow!" you reply, transfixed. Before you is a powerhouse. Light emanates off his powder-blue skin. He is adorned in leopard skin, a topknot, and a moon crown. "Shiva, do you have special powers?"

"Why yes I do! I am the most 'auspicious one' in Sanskrit, meaning I bring luck. I can either protect, destroy, or release you."

"Release me?"

"You know, from illusions?"

You sense that is a spiritual aspiration.

"But where are my friends? Can you help me or not?"

"Let me show you the secret universe. You will learn Hindu dances that will give you special powers. You will gain strength you will need for rescuing your friends and important missions."

Wow, you think, *how does he know so much?* You are intimidated but curious.

If you learn the dances from a real deity, turn to page 30.

If you run off and try to find Althea or your troupe, turn to page 133.

You perform, telling yourself the police will find Althea. You work through the final dance without a hitch, even though you are worried. This is how professional you are, how focused you are on dancing. You shine in the grand finale. When the show is over, Dame Moma hurries you to the dressing room.

"The impresarios want to meet you," she says. "Smile and nod at anything they say—this is a big break."

A well-dressed man and an elegant woman walk in. They look very refined and they intimidate you.

"I am Elsbeth, the head of all recruiting of talent for the European opera circuit. This is Mr. Gabriel Astruc, the booking agent. We are very impressed by your dancing—the styles are so fresh. We need someone who can perform modern dances, as well as classical ballet."

"Yes, this is her strong suit...to try new things." Dame Moma pushes you toward them. But you recoil. Something about this situation feels wrong.

Turn to the next page.

"Come with us to Italy to star in the Opera!" Elsbeth pulls you toward her and Mr. Astruc leads Dame Moma away, asking her questions about her collection of music recordings. You realize Elsbeth wants to speak with you without the Dame hearing. "You will be featured in the Princess Dance. You will be showered with praise and gifts! There will be more glorious costumes and a lot of hard work, night after night, performing for worldly audiences."

"Can my troupe come with me?" you ask. *More time to find Althea,* you're thinking.

"They are fine dancers but nothing like you," says Elsbeth. "We will be inviting stronger dancers to join you onstage. They will help you become famous everywhere in the world! But we have one question about your dance troupe," Elsbeth says, lowering her voice.

Go on to the next page.

Elsbeth looks down at a dossier of paperwork she holds, shuffling through fancy tri-folded sheets.

"We did want to see one additional performer tonight—Althea. Where is she? Why didn't she dance?"

Something about Elsbeth's voice sounds not so innocent.

You tug on your costume, thinking. Could they know where she is? Perhaps if you answer them, you will help Althea.

If you take a risk and tell Elsbeth what you know, turn to the next page.

If you do not say anything and go back to the troupe, turn to page 46.

"Althea's not here," you say to Elsbeth. "She has been kidnapped. Do you know something about it?"

"Not yet. We believe the Dame had her kidnapped, and that Althea wasn't the first. Mr. Astruc and I have been watching the Dame. We think she is recruiting dancers to spy for the Germans, maybe forcing them to. She is ruthlessly damaging lives," Elsbeth explains.

"Oh no!" you say, letting the information sink in. You remember that at the beginning of the tour, two dancers had to "go home" for different reasons. No one ever heard from them again.

"Oh, yes! She approached us because we train spies expertly, and she can fetch more money if you are already trained. We believe she insisted on you joining us because a deal was made for you to be taken!"

You gasp.

"It is good you came with us—become highly trained so you can foil her—or find Althea! End her before more of your friends are harmed," Elsbeth continues.

"My goodness." You don't know what else to say. Your dreams are important to you, but so is Althea.

Go on to the next page.

"It's time to get some rest," Elsbeth says, and points you to a luxurious bed. "Tomorrow, we train."

"But I am a dancer, not a spy…" you protest as you drift off to sleep.

Turn to the next page.

The next morning, Mr. Astruc and Elsbeth wake you up early to begin spy training.

"Margaretha, this training may save your life," Mr. Astruc tells you. "Your language talents are exceptional and you've traveled the world. You are going to be called into this war whether you like it or not, and we will prepare you."

Well, they are *experts,* you think. *It couldn't hurt to train.* It can be no more grueling than your dance training. You agree to begin.

"Welcome to the jungle!" says Elsbeth as she and Mr. Astruc lead you over a dangerous-looking bridge. "Here we begin Phase 1 of what we call Spy Bootcamp! First, we teach you how to sabotage!"

They bring you to an obstacle course in the highlands. You are surrounded by cascading waterfalls, slippery rocks, bamboo towers, and fragrant flowers. You look up and notice ropes suspended from the trees.

"I've used ropes in my dance training with the troupe, but never like this," you tell Elsbeth after you fall a few times.

"You have to think and move like a saboteur!" Elsbeth says. Over the next several days, they teach you to cut and knot rope, pick locks, put puzzles together, all while clocked by a timer filled with sand.

Turn to page 5.

For Phase 3 you learn weapons: the blade in the boot, knives, grenades, explosives, and smoke bombs.

"Think of fighting the Dame!" Mr. Astruc says when you drop a knife. You think of Althea and feel inspired to fight for her.

"Oh yes, I will do anything for my friends; I will do my best!"

"You must pick one signature weapon to be the most comfortable with," Elsbeth tells you. She shows you a poisonous hat pin, a special lipstick, a compact that expands into a ninja star.

You pick the hat pin and say, "Oh I know the ins and outs of these; my dad is a designer of the best fashion hats!" Hat pin it is!

"Actually, he is a baron," you lie. "Well, everyone called him that, but then he went broke." You tell the truth. Then you lie again. "Really, I am an orphan...I mean, I don't look Dutch—I am likely a lost Indian princess, actually."

"Margaretha, you had better learn to lie better, like an expert!" they scold you. You hope to become better at acting. You begin to believe spying is your calling. It's like a dance role but with superpowers.

"But my dance name is Mata Hari," you point out. "Can't I use a new code name?"

"You must. In all communications you will be known as H-21."

Turn to page 28.

Phase 3: Weapons

Grenades

Hat Pins

Blade in Boot

Knives

"We have located Althea through our intel," Elsbeth tells you one morning. "She is in Europe, dancing and spying for the Dame." It is time for your training to end and real life as a spy to begin. Elsbeth and Mr. Astruc look at you sternly.

"Actually, you have another option," Mr. Astruc says, knowing you want to rush off immediately to save Althea. "By now you have all the tools to bring Dame Moma down. Stop her before she recruits any other spies. She is boarding the *SS Orsova* for Australia and you could go aboard the steamship and take her down."

You are confused and tired. Do you follow the intel that leads to Althea or go after the Dame?

If you decide to head to Europe in search of Althea, turn to page 82.

If you choose to board the SS Orsova *and try and stop the Dame, turn to page 125.*

"You must come with me," states Commander Page—and you trust him. You grab the gloves and the music box and wrap them in a bundle of clothes.

"I'm ready."

He escorts you off the boat and onto the docks. He sings the whole time. When you are far enough away, he says, "I've saved you for now. This is where I leave you to continue the mission. One last thing, *Mata Hari*," he says as he walks away:

"Remember this:

Look to where blows the wind of Thor
A large ship sails on in the night range
Wherein a closed door the quarter light remains
Go to the—"

But you can't hear the last rhyme when the wind picks up. He is too far from you.

Turn to page 50.

30

You are a dancer, and to learn from the Lord of the Dance is an opportunity you cannot pass up.

Shiva begins: "First, sound off OM with me." He invites you to sit in a meditative position.

"I know the *om,* I have taken yoga classes with my dance troupe. We always laugh during this part."

"Oh no, Om is sacred! Yoga is so much MORE than that!" Shiva scowls, then starts the sound.

"Ommmmm," you open your mouth in an "O" shape for as long as you can and close it with an "m" sound.

"Now, look at me," Shiva instructs. "Imagine you are three parts, just like a statue: head, body, feet. Just like that, in life there are three layers: heaven, the abode of the gods; the world of humans; and, of course…the world of demons."

Go on to the next page.

Shiva gives you a drum to beat and starts pinching the air with his fingers and swaying in rhythm. "This is the dance of *moksha*, the highest freedom. Since there is order and disorder in life, you must seek balance between two forces. You must learn to be like a spy—and see through both sides!"

"Oh yes, I have heard about it in stories I learn about my dances."

"You learned my dances?" He looks mad.

"Sort of, is that not okay?" you ponder.

Shiva scoops you up and shakes you, the snake around his neck hissing at you. "Well, these are my dances, shouldn't *I* teach you?"

"No disrespect! We learn a lot about your culture because it is very far off and popular, especially with European socialites. They pay a lot of money to see us dance the dances you invented."

He pauses and stares at you. His gaze penetrates so deeply, you feel something shift in you. He seems to peer into your soul. "If you take from a culture or a god, you have to leave something to show you're not a cheat. Do you know what I mean, young one?"

Turn to the next page.

"I understand. I think."

"I will teach you the right way. If you learn, you can attain freedom anytime, from any circumstance. Yes, free yourself into *moksha*."

"Oh, wow, what a superpower!" you exclaim, not entirely sure how it works.

"Yes, this dance aids in psychic powers, which is a type of spying," he declares. "It can give you clairvoyance, clairaudience…"

"What are those?" you interrupt, curious.

"Well, for instance, you will be able to see Althea's whereabouts, or hear spirit voices that aren't there, or are from the realm of the dead."

You carefully mimic his every move. You pay the most attention you have ever paid, re-learning the proper swirls, movements for your hands called *mudras*. You feel so blessed to be learning from the source.

Go on to the next page.

"Now that you have learned these dances, we must go to the great Ocean, the Ocean of Milk, to make a sacrifice. Oh, to churn is to be holy."

Shiva clarifies: "We need to do this for the sacred power drink, the Amrita."

"A drink, like a potion?" you ask.

"More like honey after the bees," Shiva responds. "It is the nectar of the gods. We have to call forth some help. I am being summoned. The Ocean has been poisoned and needs us. There are going to be demons there, but also Devas—the good spirits—called in to help."

"Wow! I want to come!" Wait. But do you? It does sound dangerous.

"Are you sure? Are you spiritually and physically strong enough? It takes a lot to churn the Ocean!" Shiva explains: "We will churn it with a whole mountain, and share the work with a bunch of demons, even a snake with venom. We need all the help we can get!"

"What if we don't succeed?" you question.

"Oh, you will definitely be punished. If we fail, all hell, literally, will break loose."

If you agree to be his accomplice, turn to page 93.

If you say no because it is ridiculous, turn to page 95.

"I'm fine on my own," you say, reminding yourself to trust no one. "I don't need your help. Thanks anyway!" you yell, rushing away toward the sound of the music.

You follow the music until you discover a crowd. The celebrating people are illuminated by lit torches. Incense fills the air, colored banners flash, small effigies are lit up. A parade! Larger-than-life puppets with horned heads, bulging eyeballs, and flame-painted wings charge down the street. They are so frightening!

Dame Moma told you stories about these creatures. They are *Ogoh-ogoh,* and it is the eve of the Balinese New Year, the Nyepi Festival. This is what kept the local band from performing for your dance tonight. Many Balinese stream by, banging on drums, dressed alike in gold, balancing fruit towers on their heads.

Turn to page 36.

You get shuffled around in the crowd. It's stifling. You look around for any signs of Althea in all of the colors and chaos.

A troupe of monkeys wearing small golden hats approach you in the street, carrying lit sparklers. They jangle around, doing flips and acrobatics. One of the monkeys swings off from formation and jumps onto your arm, startling you. He stares you right in the eyes and kisses the middle of your forehead. He hands you his sparkler.

"See? You shine! You are heavenly—follow me!" He speaks!

Go on to the next page.

Then, nearby, a loud firework pops off.

"EEK!" you scream, your nerves raw from the events of the evening. The monkey does not flinch. He curves a creepy finger at you and then toward himself. You don't know what to do.

If you run off the main road into the jungle to safety, turn to page 15.

If you want to stay in the parade, turn to page 39.

If you follow the odd monkey, no matter the cost, turn to page 51.

You stay in the festival and become enthralled by huge demons with grotesque features, as if you are walking in a nightmare. Then, you see sparkling dancers, glittering from head to toe. You approach these ethereal creatures that seem to be dancing and floating at the same time. You gawk at their beauty. They surround you and sing:

"The goddess. The goddess. We celestial nymphs, arise out of the ocean of bliss, of bliss, in service of the goddess…"

"You remind me of my dance troupe. Can I dance with you?"

"Yes, join us! You too are a dancing Apsara. We are all the Daughters of Joy." They giggle. You dance the night away, closing your eyes in a trance, visions of new worlds decorating the back of your eyelids.

"Woooooooooo!" you sing and spin, getting dizzy.

"Oh," they moan. "We just love your moves." You feel at home, so free to move. However—you are not on stage!

Turn to the next page.

40

You chirp with song and you dance, bonding with them.

"We are strong, we protect the goddess, we hurt those in her way. Say, we will help you, too, sister. You are one of us!" *Smooch!* They group hug you. Their energy is smothering. Alarmed, you shove them and step back quickly.

You accidentally smash some offerings: petals, crystals, a sacrificial doll. The joy shifts to terror. They ramp up their dancing and whirling and spinning. They sneer and spit on you—some are even frothing at the mouth! The Apsaras circle around you as if you are in trouble. Your dance troupe doesn't act sour like this. What will you do?

"Punish the perpetrator!" You must have committed a major religious *faux pas!* They howl and lunge for you.

If you decide to protect yourself, turn to page 65.

If you try to escape, turn to page 69.

"You must give me back my fashion!" You think quickly to demand your luggage. If you can get the gloves, you can use them on him and try to escape. "I won't leave until I have it!"

Finally, the commander leaves and comes out, dragging your trunk. He taps it, motioning to it with a pleading look. "You can grab a few items."

He seems to know something; you wonder: *Maybe he is on the German side and this is supposed to happen...or maybe this commander is who the truth serum is meant for.*

Either way, you carefully open your luggage and check to see whether the serum gloves are still there. Then you notice a small, ornate music box protected by your fur collar. *Did the commander put that in there? Is he with me or against me?* you contemplate in your head.

If you must find out more about the music box, turn to page 29.

If you believe you should use the gloves now, turn to page 122.

You step up to the temple. Its entryway starts glowing and you feel incredibly calm. After a few minutes, you hear dull chanting. Suddenly, out of nowhere, smoke swirls in out of the ether, forming into the shape of a floating eye. A voice speaks loudly:

"Look into the Mystical Eye." It is illuminated. You are transfixed. "The Eye is a Spy!" the voice shouts, shattering the smoke drawing. You shake upright and hear an object bouncing. All that is left is a hefty eye-shaped coin with a glowing pupil and iris figure etched on it.

"With this third eye, the all-seeing-eye, you possess knowledge infinite. All that is unseen, and alive into eternity. Whenever you rub it, this bestows the forces of Sun, Moon, and Fire upon you. To aid you. For you are a child of the Light. And your mission has begun."

"Mission?"

"To help others. To save them from darkness, show them the light. After all, we pick you because Mata Hari means 'Eye of the Sun.'"

"Yes, that is me! Indeed. Will I be able to find Althea?"

"The power is yours!" The voice fades through the incense.

Turn to the next page.

44

"Please take it." A towering blue and black female-shaped creature with a necklace of skulls appears before you. She is imposing. You lose your breath. This might be the end! But surprisingly, she has a soothing voice. Arising, with bloody lips, she says:

"Hello, Mata. Welcome. I am Kali, the Hindu goddess of creation and destruction. I am worshipped all over. This is my home. You must worship me."

"Thank you for having me. It is so intricate and pretty here, but I do not know how to worship."

"Simply surrender. Just relax." You try to relax your body. "Do it!" she insists. You try to relax even more, but her extreme energy is making you tense.

"Do not resist me—I am the mighty mother goddess!" she roars. "You are my daughter, come with me NOW! Bring the coin!" She lunges at you with long, dagger-like fingernails. The rattling necklace of skulls whips into your face.

"Don't be frightened now that you are with me. You must decide; which side of me would you like to see? Kali-the-Mother or Kali-the-Destroyer?"

"Both sound so amazing!" you say quickly, because you do not want to upset her.

"Well," she explains, "though having a form, I am formless; I am without beginning, without end. I am Creatrix, Protectress, and Destructress."

"Huh?" you ask, perplexed.

Turn to page 117.

You tell Elsbeth that you appreciate her offer, but you believe that you will find greater success if you stay with your dance troupe. You tell her nothing about Althea.

The next morning, you sneak away for an early walk. Pink hues of dawn tickle your surroundings with peachy rose colors. You feel serene and peaceful as you walk on the beach. Still, all of your senses are on, as you look for clues.

You reach the water at sunrise. A team of dolphins appear, laughing and dancing together. The waves call you to jump in, and you do. You play with the dolphins, forgetting all your troubles…

The waves lap and crash. You are often pulled under but bob back up, unafraid and spitting out salt water. An enormous wave descends, and you grab on to a dolphin's back, clutching around its neck. The wave is out of control, and you are sucked under. You hold on to your dolphin friend with all your might.

You and the dolphin push into deep, dark water. *This must be a rip tide,* you think. Even the dolphin seems tense and frightened. You spin and whirl through the dark surging pocket. You open your eyes and see a constellation of lights shooting by. This isn't a rip tide. What's happening?

When you and the dolphin resurface, you feel something has changed. You look around. You don't know where you are. You are definitely in colder, less friendly waters.

Turn to page 48.

"Help!" you yell, shivering and gasping for air, skimming the surface on the back of the dolphin.

Just when you are about to panic, you spot a boat, submerged in the water. It has a long arm shooting straight up with a hole like an eye at the end. You motion to the dolphin to quickly dive down and explore—you see an oblong hunk of shining metal, with small windows.

When you get closer to the peephole, you swear you see Althea waving inside. You've never seen this type of boat before—it's a submarine. One of the girls in your dance troupe, whose dad is a top general from America, told you all about the new war machines. Loud sounds reverberate. When you bound to the surface again, there are bombs dropping in the water.

Should you get to land where you can regroup, but might face a battle? If so, turn to page 73.

Or should you command the dolphin to chase the submarine through the cold waters? If so, turn to page 104.

50

You try to memorize the song as you rush to open the music box. You turn the small crank. At first nothing happens, and you think it must be broken, but after three full cranks clockwise a song plays and a panel pops open. You see a document wedged in the box. You realize the paper was kept hidden in the "broken" music for a reason. It is a secret message.

Turn to page 11.

You follow the monkey away from the parade. He leaps to the left and right, telling you stories.

"Who—or what—are you?" you ask.

"I am Hanuman! It is the festival of clearing the dead for the New Year. You saw the *Ogoh-ogoh* out there, the spirits of evil. Everyone here lets the evil live! For the light to thrive, there is dark. We must have both good and evil in life, right?"

"That makes sense!" you say.

"When I saw you at the festival—I knew you were The One!" he laughs, pointing at you and jumping up and down. "However," the monkey continues, "for now, we also need your friend to activate the New Year. We need both of you!"

"What do you mean?" you ask, intrigued.

"Althea's name means 'healing' and it is she that we need for the most important part of the festival."

"Wait, you've seen Althea? Where is she?!!"

Turn to the next page.

Hanuman doesn't answer you.

"Tomorrow the whole island remains silent in tribute to our gods. We need her and the Eye of the Dawn to activate the healing! She cannot help us until she sees you. You must come now. I promise to help you return to your friends."

You stay quiet and follow the talking monkey. He's bouncing along, back to telling you wild stories. "When I was a child, I grabbed the sun, mistaking it for a fruit. Indra the lightning god had to throw bolts to stop me."

You say, "You have led a very exciting life. But, please explain, what did you mean by tribute? I have to make sure Althea is not being sacrificed."

"Well, come into the temple to find out!" he teases in a thundering voice.

"I thought that's where we were going!" you answer.

"Ah," he replies, smiling, "but it's so much more than the destination. It is the journey."

After a long, winding stretch in the jungle, Hanuman leads you through the clouds to an ornate temple. Before you are numerous stone buildings layered with flights of stairs, large bells, small waterfalls, and a plaza. The columns are painted with gold flowers.

There are splotches that look like blood on the temple plaza.

Turn to page 54.

54

Hanuman sees you looking at them.

"Oh yeah, that is probably from some sacrifices. For Kali. She likes blood."

You frown. *What have I gotten myself into?*

"Kali can create problems for travelers such as yourself. Entrance into the main temple is tricky—I know because I myself am a trickster! You must charm Ganesha, the wise but greedy elephant guard. If you are not of pure mind and soul, you will not be allowed admittance."

"That is a lot to consider!" You stare at the monkey quizzically. You look up to see an elephant with a large-bellied, more-human-than-elephant body guarding the main temple gates. He looks well-fed and has four arms—one holds a broken tusk.

"Is Althea in there?" you ask.

Hanuman only responds in a riddle: "Only you, who it is up to, will find the other you. I know of a small crypt that *may* have an entrance. But it may not. You must pick."

You do not know if either of these choices is a route to Althea. And Hanuman said you may not be ready to enter. What if you make a decision that leads to sacrifice, for you or for Althea?

If you decide to try to enter the temple, facing whatever scary Kali has in store, go on to the next page.

If you decide to follow the monkey into a smaller crypt building, in hopes he will continue to help you, turn to page 123.

You don't know if the temple will be serene or operate like a trap. The complex has a huge spread of stone formations. Any of these buildings could be dangerous, any could hold a key. The main temple looks so gorgeous, decorated with ornate carvings of animals and flowers and flame shapes.

You look for any other entrances to the temple besides the main one. At every turn, there is a new distraction.

A gold peacock struts by and you pet it. It bites you. *Ouch!* Then, you discover a pot of rice. You eat it, you are so hungry. It turns you green and sickly. When you try to recover in some shade, you are struck by a falling coconut. You feel so dazed and defeated walking around the complex, knocking on doors that refuse to open.

"I know! I will find an offering, something to appease the gods." You start over, looking for ideas of what to offer. Just when everything feels hopeless, a mouse scurries over your feet.

"Ack!" You jump back!

It looks up at you, scrunching its teeny nose, and tells you, "Approach the elephant now. I am his friend. I talked to him. Now is the moment."

Turn to the next page.

56

"You are such a wondermouse!" The mouse leads you to Ganesha, who is perched on the beautiful petals of a lotus flower like a king on a throne. "I still can't seem to gain entry, help me?" you sob.

"I am Ganesha, I will remove all obstacles, everyone prays to me—"

"Great, help me!" you beg, interrupting.

"—for everyday help."

"I am facing so many obstacles!" you sob.

"—Mata, you are not listening. Listen up or another curse will befall you! First, you must smash a coconut and make me a prayer."

"A coconut! Of course!" you reply, rushing around to find the one that put a gnash on your head.

"No, a fresh one, silly," he insists, so you climb a coconut tree. "Oh, and get one for yourself!" He yells. You fetch them, and he opens them on his broken tusk. As you drink yours, your skin returns to normal and your wound heals. You feel suddenly psychic.

Turn to page 58.

58

"Look into my eyes. Meditate, concentrate. Now close your eyes, get quiet, I will ask you questions. Answer with the first phrase that comes to mind. Don't overthink it. The answer is right in front of you. What are my large ears for?" he asks.

"To hear everything?" The answer seems to shoot out right from your gut.

"What is my large head for?"

"To know more, oh wise one."

"Correct! What about my huge stomach?"

"To digest all the good and all the bad. To make energy."

"Yes! In my right hand is my broken tusk. What does it represent?"

"Ouch!" You scrunch your closed eyes, feeling the loss.

"That is what I wrote the epic poem with. In my lower left hand is a treasure…"

"Candy! Can I have it?"

"Mata—focus! What is the rope for?"

Go on to the next page.

"To pull one toward their goals?" You open one eye, unsure.

"What is the axe for?"

"To cut all bonds!" You squeeze your eyelids and wait.

"What is the mouse for?"

"Uh, to help me?" you guess, losing concentration. Still, you are learning symbolism you never knew.

"Close enough!" Ganesha opens the gate. "You may enter the temple."

To finally enter the sacred temple, turn to page 43.

To keep learning from the wisdom of Ganesha, turn to page 91.

"Farewell, Paris, do not forget me. I shall return," you say, sobbing dramatically from your seat on the train. At least you are finally to be reunited with your best friend! You arrive in Berlin, another exciting city. You meet Althea at the Alexanderplatz, the central transit station.

"Althea?" you cry, and you embrace each other. You catch up on all that's happened while you have been apart, and how both of you have turned from a life of dance to a life of spying.

You and Althea ride around on the brand-new electric tram, looking for Museum Island, where you are to rehearse your assignment.

"The tram is so weird!" Althea notices. It's connected to the railway by a wire and powered by electricity. It rattles a lot and you are so busy laughing with your pal, you get lost in the city.

"We haven't passed any water," Althea says, nervously.

"We are looking for an island," you tell the driver. "Museum Island? Do you know it?"

"Ah, it is not an island; it is just several museums near each other," he says. He tells you which tram to take to reach it.

When you arrive at the "island" of museums, you are greeted by a man in a suit and tails and a woman wearing large eyeglasses, who are expecting you. You don't know who is a performer and who is a spy. You stare in awe at the grand collection of artifacts as you are rushed past them.

Turn to the next page.

You turn back to Althea, suddenly feeling panic. "We need to practice tap for tonight—I don't know how to do it!"

"No one does. Just think of the European Jig a bit, and the weight of your Dutch clogs. Front-toe heel. Front-toe heel. Repeat." You work on long and short sounds to mimic the "dah-dit" of Morse Code. Before you know it, the performance is upon you.

"Meet in the kitchen," the woman with eyeglasses whispers to you both before you go out onstage, and you and Althea nod. It's the first message you will tap to those in the know.

"Welcome to the Ambassadors' Ball!" the emcee announces with glee. "It's a very special night! We have brought the latest dance sensation! They will be performing *Night Stars,* to showcase tap dance—the jazz dance from America. It is our honor to introduce, Althea...and the star, Mata Hari!"

Go on to the next page.

The crowd roars; blinding lights designed to sparkle like stars come on. You try to click for long-short-long sounds that spell out: *Meet in the kitchen*.

Lights keep flashing. You can't keep up. You and Althea are not in sync.

-- . .- - / .. -. / ... - .. -.- -.-

M-E-A-T- I-N S-T-I-C-K, you tap out by accident.

You look at each other, admitting with your eyes that you are way out of your league. Althea runs offstage crying, and you finish the number alone before finding her backstage.

"Althea! Who cares if we messed up? We can still complete our mission," you whisper. You must find Ladoux. You see him talking to a German officer. You know they are plotting something. You walk by with a confident attitude, eavesdropping on their conversation.

You stand very close to the two men.

"Hello sirs," you say, first in French and then in German. "We have chosen to show you all the props and costumes we travel with—back there. You will be our special guests!"

"Stop bothering me, brat." It didn't work.

Turn to the next page.

Althea hangs back, looking awkward. You have to think quickly. Time is running out. The two men approach the kitchen.

You thrust out your hand, yank Ladoux's gold pocket watch off his chest, and run.

He follows, faster than you expected. You dash to the kitchen, where at least one person on your side will be waiting. You hope.

But Ladoux chases you into an empty kitchen and catches you quickly. He pins you against the kitchen stove.

You punch him, knee his groin, then kick your tap shoe into his stomach.

"Ouf! I'll get you!"

French intelligence officers finally arrive to your aid. Guns are drawn. You dash into the food cooler, stepping into the cold, large ice box. You are just in time. Shots are fired. You shift the shelf up and escape into a hallway.

The passageway is so dark that you have to trust your gut. You see a shaft of light at one end filled with construction dust. It must lead to an exhibition. You want to see Nefertiti, because you know she may inspire you with power. Why not? You're safe now, right?

If you decide to explore the museum, turn to page 70.

If you think you should run away as far as possible, turn to page 130.

"Oh, please don't be mad at me. I have an enemy! Help me find Althea's kidnappers." You try to reason with them, tell them about the kidnapping. "Remember, I am like a sister. I need help."

The Daughters are spinning so fast, you cannot see them. They cannot hear you. They are completely transformed. You try to escape the circle. But it is too late. Staying with the Daughters of Joy was a mistake. The frenzy turns sacrificial and they make it known you are their victim.

The End

66

The next day, you board the luxury liner *SS Orsova,* Third Class. You pose as a waiter in a uniform and moustache. You stand among other workers and immigrants on their way to a new life in Australia. You nervously reach the second tier for Second Class, where your dance troupe mingles with the upper class in lavish dining rooms and a ballroom with a lively band.

You get to work and blend in with the staff. This way, you will have access to First Class, where the Dame is. You scope her cabin, 6C, for access to her room; you learn her routine and stalk the entertainment schedules. No one suspects you.

Turn to page 68.

You serve dinner to the table next to your dance troupe. It's difficult to hear their happy conversations and not be able to say who you are or warn them that they are in danger.

When the Dame is out for dinner, you are able to disguise as room service but have to pick the lock on her cabin. You locate the documents and add invisible ink. You manage to scurry off before she returns. Phew!

The second part will be much harder; she never leaves her cane, even in her sleep. Maybe now is the time to show yourself to the troupe, and ask their help. But it would put them in danger, and maybe you. They could be loyal to the Dame.

If you fly solo for the final act of sabotage, turn to page 108.

If you decide to enlist some friends, putting them at risk, turn to page 129.

"I'll show you some moves! Wild grooves you've never seen!" you croon to them. Then you start squealing and clawing on the ground, churning up dirt to create a distraction. With so many flailing limbs mixed in with dust, your vision is impaired, but you dart away.

You come up with a plan for what you will say. You will apologize for running from the show. *I'm sorry, I was just so nervous. Do not think I am bad,* you will tell them.

You nestle yourself into bed. Just as dawn is breaking, you laugh to yourself, satisfied. *After all,* you think, *my stage name means "Eye of the Dawn."* You laugh at how you escaped the frenzy. You close your eyes, thinking of the memorable night you had.

The End

70

You cannot help it—experiencing the museum exhibits are too enticing. You follow the dust and find a door—there is a lot under construction. Still, the artifacts and sculptures beckon you. You see gems you have read about in ancient history: the lion gates of Ishtar, the Pergamon building, frescos of Athena and Zeus. Your favorite is the bust of Nefertiti, the great Egyptian queen. You wonder how the Germans acquired the cradle of old civilization. You are in awe.

As you walk into the main atrium, the moonlight showers down on you. It swims through the ceiling, lighting up the statues in a glow. You start to dance, gliding around the figures. Whispering to your spiritual ancestors, "Help me." You feel the ancients giving you strength. It is time to continue on.

Turn to page 72.

72

You exit the museum and rush past several others, just in time to catch the last train back to Paris. You don't know what happened to Ladoux. You hope they caught him or even shot him. Maybe you'll still receive a medal of honor?

"I'm exhausted!" you say to no one as you search for the sleeper cabin. But then you see a familiar man aboard the train with you. Ladoux! He stands down the train car, looking around it wild-eyed, and walks in your direction.

Oh no! How did he escape arrest? Did he follow you? Either way you are terrified, and in danger.

You could leap from the train right now while it's moving. You might get injured, and he might follow you. If you stay aboard, he could hurt you on the train. But, if you stay on, you could possibly lead him right back to the authorities for arrest. *Remember the camoufleurs,* you recall from your spy training, when you learned about women who developed new camouflaging techniques. *Hmm... well, if he follows me, I can hide and catch him instead!*

If you continue by train and lure Ladoux to the authorities, turn to page 102.

If you jump off the train, turn to page 126.

You are in the middle of a battle, and it is not safe in the water!

Bombs drop all around you, but you ride the dolphin to land. You arrive, barely breathing, on the shore. "Goodbye, dolphin friend, be safe out there, find that portal quickly back to your home." You wish you were back in Bali, before all this badness. You pass out from exhaustion on the beach.

Turn to the next page.

74

You are transported to a makeshift clinic on the Western Front. You have whiplash, hypothermia, and a knee injury…that really frightens you because you need healthy joints for dancing.

You are in France, in an area called Champagne, in the middle of a raging battle. In the war zone, you are surrounded by massive trenches, battalions, blown up ground, and bombs. The allies are downtrodden, the Western Front is not faring well. There are only iron rations to eat: gritty barley, tough biscuits, and sometimes bacon. It is bleak.

"I know!" you announce when you are recovered. "I will perform the very colorful Butterfly Dance to help. It will rally the troops; it always lifts the mood of everyone who sees it."

You take gauze and cotton strips from the nurses and dye them with teas. You stitch them together to make a costume. You dance as if you fly and flit, cheered on by the soldiers. You are positive you are bringing good cheer and healing.

Turn to page 76.

76

Afterward, you are cooling off and wrapping your knee when some generals approach. They corner you.

"We saw what you did," a general tells you. They are fuming mad.

"What are you talking about?"

"We saw the messages you were sending when you were dancing! Who was it for?" They accuse you of espionage.

"Wait, what? You are mistaken! I am but a butterfly in the sun, spreading colors...but I beg you to believe me. I have never committed an act of espionage against France. Never. Never."

France is not doing well in battle, morale is low, and they need a scapegoat.

"Mata Hari, you are accused of sending secret messages through your dance movements," says the general. They threaten to arrest you! The punishment for espionage is death.

"You have three choices to avoid a trial: go home, go to live with the faithful nuns, or stay with the nurses and be dutiful."

If you return to your hometown and stay out of the war, turn to page 79.

If you decide to join the nuns, turn to page 128.

If you stay and help the nurses, turn to page 98.

You figure out that:

JRWRWKHVKRUH=GOTOTHESHORE.

Here you are, right at the shore already. You remember the rhyme Commander Page spoke:

Look to where blows the wind of Thor
A large ship sails on in the night range

The direction to go to the shore seems clear, but there is also a second line of jumbled letters. You use the code and the alphabet in the same way: three shifts to the right to crack the code. Find each letter in the code and, using the real alphabet, fill in the rest of the blanks below! Use the decoder from page 14 to help crack this code.

J	R	W	R	W	K	H	J	U	D	Q	J	H
G			O			E						

Turn to page 119.

At first, when you get home to Leeuwarden, you are so happy to see your family. You speak in your favorite language, Frisian, the language of your people. But small-town Netherlands feels bland. You teach at the girls' school for learning, where you rebel by wearing a red dress, causing a scandal. You are an orchid among buttercups.

Your father, a well-known hat maker, buys you a one-of-a-kind goat-driven carriage. You give friends rides like a charioteer along the canals and brick streets. You continue learning languages. Keeping poetry scrapbooks is a popular pastime, so you collect and send them to your dancer friends. You check the post office near your flat for any replies, but none come. You are lonely.

Turn to the next page.

You pick up the routines of your old life, spending time at the Waag, an old weigh house for Dutch trading that dates back to 1600s. A popular stop on the canal trading routes, people from all over gather there. You see an old family friend there, Herr Kramer, who is an important merchant.

"Mata, I know you are stifled here. I work for the German secret service. I can offer you 20,000 francs, new dresses, and passage out of Leeuwarden, but I need a favor. We need you to intercept information in Spain for the benefit of Germany in the war."

"I would love to escape this boring tomb!"

He gives you some money, gloves soaked in truth serum, and disappearing ink, as well as a new falsified passport.

"Being from a neutral nation like the Netherlands, you are always able to travel across borders," says Herr Kramer. "But the war has made it much harder. You cannot travel directly to Spain, due to the boundaries of the war zones. You will travel by ship via England. Take this parcel also, but do not open it until you are onboard. Your instructions are inside."

"Finally, some fun!" you say. But then you pause. Your time traveling abroad has shaped your opinions about this war, and both you and the people you've trusted along the way have not sided with Germany.

If you accept the bribe to spy for Germany, go on to the next page.

If you refuse the mission, turn to page 103.

You arrive in Portsmouth, England, after your travel by sea. Officers storm onboard when you dock, surrounding you.

"Show us your papers," they command. You scrounge around for the ones Herr Kramer gave you to use. They burn the papers and confiscate your luggage. "You are the spy Clara Benedix!" they assert, calling you by the name on your fake documents.

"No, I am not!" You claim innocence, but no one cares. Everyone has spy fever, and many women are being accused and arrested.

"Commander Page will be taking you to Scotland Yard for interrogation," the officers say as they drag you off the comforts of the ship to the docks. Oh no, that is the notorious London police station!

Turn to page 41.

"Isn't this just exquisite?" you exclaim when you arrive at La Scala theater in Milan. You marvel at the Italian architecture, velvet red cushions, and golden box seats. You perform your heart out under chandeliers. On your days off you are shopping and eating the finest food, but it is still so much work. Your feet are calloused. You receive many new gifts and add them to your "princess of the world" costumes, always dripping in expensive fabrics, jewels, and cascading flowers. After several weeks performing and wowing audiences, the papers are abuzz, hailing your talent as a star.

You almost forget about Althea. As do the recruiters. They have you where they want you—you are making them money. You are more famous than ever.

Finally, you are invited to perform in Paris, the city of your dreams.

Turn to page 84.

84

You arrive in Paris with hordes of fans tremendously excited to see you. You are agog with celebrity. It is the end of the *Belle Époque,* meaning "Beautiful Era." Paris is full of glamour, rich aristocrats, and a cultural explosion of salons, cabarets, restaurants, and museums. Yet war rations and the losses of World War I are destroying this exuberance and innocence.

Elsbeth and Mr. Astruc give you a tour of Paris, a city they've been to many times.

"Look, there is the Eiffel Tower on the Champ de Mars," Elsbeth tells you. "It was built for the World's Fair of 1889—many people did not like it! It was shining and surprising and made everyone feel awe, but it was very controversial. People thought it was ugly and it was almost destroyed. A radio antenna is what saved the tower. It can monitor the transmissions of war communications."

Turn to page 86.

"Tonight we are going to a very grand party, where you will be introduced to high society," Elsbeth says.

"Perfect!" you agree.

"All the great socialites will be there. Be on your best behavior; listen closely," Mr. Astruc instructs.

Elsbeth and Mr. Astruc take you to a castle that is the home of Monsieur Émile Guimet, a wealthy collector of art.

"Welcome. Welcome. Mata Hari! What an honor," the Monsieur greets you. Inside is a stunning array of Asian and Indian art. You recognize Buddhist and Hindu statues from your travels. He lends you armbands, a breastplate, and a headdress from the collection for your costume!

"Come see the library, where you will perform." You are escorted to a gorgeous room filled with art and books, as well as the most fascinating aristocrats of Paris. Smart, fashionable women, the chocolatier Meunier, Molier the circus artist, the composer Jules Massenet, the Baron Henri de Rothschild, and Jules Cambon, the head of the Foreign Ministry, all smile at you.

You perform the dazzling dance of Inanna, a Sumerian goddess, wowing everyone. You bask in your popularity as the elite shower you with flattery: "You are very talented. We adore you!" They encircle you with admiration.

Go on to the next page.

"*Merci. Merci!*" You speak in your very best French. "My dance is a sacred poem in which each movement is a word. And every word is underlined by music," you wax poetic, trying to impress them. Cambon pulls you aside with urgency.

"Mata Hari, France needs a favor," Cambon tells you. "We are on the good side of the war. You must trap one of our own, George Ladoux, the head of our Bureau of Counterespionage. He has turned on us and given out important intel to the enemy. He is giving the other side our secrets!"

"Bureau? What is that? Like a bureau where you keep clothes?"

"It is a place in France where we spy on the spies. We gather intel to keep our soldiers safe. Ladoux is a traitor, spying for the enemy! We need evidence to imprison him."

"What does it require?"

"We will send you to Berlin, where you will gather intel on Ladoux by attending the Ambassadors' Ball and performing. We will train you to use tap dancing to send secret messages in Morse Code once you have the information we need. We will also reunite you with your friend Althea!"

To find out more about the Ambassadors' Ball with Althea, turn to the next page.

Or if you decide not to get involved...and hope to perform in Paris, turn to page 96.

88

"Oh right, yes, I want to be reunited with Althea. But why will we go to Germany?" you press them. "And I don't know tap dancing, is that like clogging?"

"Usually our spies do not ask so many questions," says Cambon. "Germany is where all the officials will gather and Ladoux will be sharing intel with our enemies. And tap dancing, like Morse Code, creates simple long and short sounds. We will give you the shoes with metal taps on them to make the sounds. It's a rhythmic dance from America. A mix of clogging and the Juba dance.

"Now, the Ball will take place in the Pergamon Museum, which is new and under construction. If there is danger, you can slip to safety through the huge ice box. That will lead you through to the museum's exit."

"The ice box?" you are not sure. All of this sounds so unfamiliar.

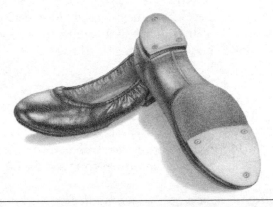

Go on to the next page.

"Our people have already worked something out with this food cooler and it will have a trap door to escape through. Now, listen closely. You could get squeezed, trapped, or even freeze to death in there. Quickly, you must pull the largest shelf; it will shift into an opening that will lead you to a secret hallway."

"Will this mission make me famous?" you ask. You are leaving so much behind.

"Yes, there is a Medal of Honor in it for you!"

"Hmmm," you mutter. You have enjoyed Paris, and not felt any of the danger and uncertainty Cambon describes.

Turn to the next page.

"Well, I do love learning new dances. An American one at that! But, gosh, it is so new. At least I know Morse Code," you say, hoping you remember it well enough from your training.

"Tap is brand new to Europe! You will be among the first to dance it here."

Being the first tap dancer in Europe excites you, but you usually have more time to perfect new dances. Could you harm the reputation of your talent if you try this brand-new dance for the first time under pressure?

If you accept the mission to the Ambassadors'
Ball, turn to page 61.

If you decide to reject the assignment because
you cannot tap, turn to page 132.

You decide to be wise and learn from Ganesha, the god of wisdom. This doesn't go so well, though, because it is like wisdom overload. At first, your circuits spaz out. You are just human after all. But then, after months of learning and gaining knowledge, your circuits fire, your humanness expands and expands until you are beyond human. You learn all the traditions, religions, and spirit sciences. You continue to learn stories, symbols, alphabets, and wisdom's traditions. Hoping to write an epic poem like him. And it's bliss.

The End

You and Shiva transport without any problems to a huge, sweeping coast. He is powered by so much wisdom and energy. Before you is an Ocean so vast it has no boundaries—at one with the great cosmos. Shiva seems happy to be there. He announces: "In order to churn the ocean, the frothy milk, I must call forth some friends. And enemies."

The good spirits, the Devas, flutter in. Then bad spirits, the Demons, show up.

Turn to the next page.

"Now, this is how we do the churning." Shiva chants a few Sanskrit spells. Huge swaths of the ocean curl and capsize. You are churning with your whole body, dancing in place among the others, when the ocean starts to froth like steamed milk. "All sorts of gifts will erupt out of it," Shiva says.

You keep dancing in place to churn it, even though you are extremely tired.

"Wow, look at these omens!" you exclaim as they are brought up from the depths: the moon erupts, then the celestial dancers, a grand horse, a conch, a magic bow, a perfume tree. You churn for an eternity, yielding a sacred cow and cascading gems and jewels. Then, the physician of the gods emerges, carrying the treasure, the Amrita drink! Just as you reach for it, you are consumed with frothing seawater. Indeed, you drown from exhaustion. The ocean absorbs you.

The End

"BUT I AM THE SUPREME BEING! You cannot refuse me!" Shiva shouts. He is so irate his skin starts to boil. His head turns into a thousand heads and twice as many eyes. You are terrified. The earth shakes. Rains descend. "I am all the elements! Without the dances, I shall be formless.

"Without passing on the dances, there is no point, there is no way to order the universe! I must now destroy Time! All physical realities exist within the span of Time. When I do this, everything is over."

And with one jarring dance move, Shiva swings and thrusts his body. He shatters Time. All turns to jelly. You can only see a great blur. Time is destroyed. You are destroyed.

The End

96

You decide to not get further involved with counterespionage; instead, you go happily gallivanting down the Champs-Élysées, and then decide to find the Paris Opera, a place you have always been obsessed with since you were a child. You stumble down smaller side streets where everything is ornamented in the art nouveau style. When you are near the Opera House, you see a small, mysterious shop titled in scrolling letters: THE SHOP OF THE MARVELOUS.

An elegant bohemian woman stands in the doorway and beckons you. "I know who you are, Mata. Enter here for your destiny."

Turn to page 99.

You decide to stay with the nurses. You want to help them. Healing injury becomes your life: broken hearts and bones, gassed lungs, shell shock, cooties, typhoid fever, and trench foot.

You learn to dress wounds, to give bed baths; you endlessly mend and patch and set casts. You find yourself staring into the wounds. They are like gaping calderas left over from a volcano, loaded with blood and pus, scabs and scars.

"This is unnecessary pain!" you tell a fellow nurse, Linda, sadly.

"The word 'souvenir' was coined to define the scars of war," she tells you.

"Some souvenirs," you mutter. Sometimes the wounds turn black and necrotic. Limbs are amputated in front of you. Many lives are lost. You cry yourself to sleep from all the horror. You wish for peace.

There are just so many deaths. The war will take over 16 million. You and your fellow nurses do not win the fight against death. Death surrounds you. It overcomes you.

The End

"My name is Pixie," says the shopkeeper in an English accent.

"A pleasure to meet you," you tell her. You are immediately drawn into the store. It is like a forbidden world. Altars are set against hanging lace tapestries, and candles line the wall. Multiple crystals stand at attention on the shelves, and there is a huge symbol painted on the floor. Cards with illustrations on them litter a round table. She gestures to the cards.

"These are my tarot cards. I am the artist, the Witch-in-Residence." As you stand there, a tarantula crawls onto her shoulder.

"Pixie, there is a spider on you!"

"Oh, this is my friend, Grandmother Storyteller." Pixie points to a pile of cards. "One of these cards will determine where to go to elevate yourself, to become more famous. That is what you are in Paris for, correct?"

Turn to page 101.

"Correct," you respond, but offer nothing further. You know the trick against false mediums: say very little, as anything you reveal will be used to describe your destiny.

Pixie points to two opposite cards.

"Choose a card. If you choose the one on the right, you are meant to continue on with me. If you choose the left card, the journey you will take will be alone. Decide if being independent and brave will bring you fame. The decision is your will, but the message from the cards is the fate of the universe. Whichever card you pick, that is destined. What will it be, Mata?"

If you choose to flip the one on the right and work with Pixie, turn to page 105.

If you choose the one on the left to learn about a solo journey, turn to page 109.

You stay on the train, saving your legs and ankles from any harm. You dart between train cars, looking for a place to hide from Ladoux. The dining car is filled with people. Maybe you should inform someone. A fancy-hatted lady notices your frightened face. She gestures beside her.

"Can I hide?" you ask her. She does not speak any languages you do, so you gesture down between her heavy skirts and the table. She nods. You crouch below the table, hidden by her skirts.

You position yourself well enough so that you can still see the doors. You take out your special hat pin, loaded with poison.

You decide to take down Ladoux before he can hurt you. If you strike him with your hat pin, he will at least be rendered unconscious. Then the train police can arrest him.

Ladoux steps into the dining car, swaying as the train jangles around a bend. He stands close to your table. He is close enough, but you are not sure of your aim. You plunge the hat pin into his leg. He falls down. The puncture is too deep. Ladoux dies.

When the train finally reaches Paris, all of France rolls out the red carpet for you. "Mata Hari, Mata Hari, hero of the war!" the people shout as you are treated like a queen and happily receive your Medal of Honor.

The End

You leave the Waag and dump all the disappearing ink in the canals. You refuse to help a cause you don't believe in, or to live in a web of lies!

But you are so bored in your small hometown, you find yourself lying anyway. Small lies, medium ones, then huge ones—just to make the time pass. You lose friends from your lying. The gray weather does not help. You make the best of it, reading at the café. You say you are making a scavenger game spotting lion heads above doorways all over town, but you are mapping all the canals: the exits out of town. You hatch a plan.

One day, you head down to the boats and hide in one, hoping it will take you back to Paris. Only the boat is going nowhere. Days pass. Complete boredom overcomes you as you suffocate from *ennui,* the French word that means "complete boredom." *Perhaps this is peace,* you muse. You become bored to death.

The End

You swim around the U-boat marked SM U-20. You realize quickly there is no way to get in. You wave at Althea. She cannot escape. The dolphin circles around, also trying. You pound on it. Rescuing her is futile. You run out of energy.

When you surface, in the distance is a shimmering set of graphics. There are squares and rectangles floating on the ocean! The dolphin takes you closer, but you cannot tell exactly how large or where it is. The shapes of the paint must be confusing to an enemy on purpose. Dolphin sonar finds the ship, finally. You are freezing, wishing you were coated in dolphin blubber.

When you arrive, you see cargo and know it is a friendly navy boat, the *Euterpe*. They are allies, but it is too late. You are frozen.

The End

You choose the card on the right side. It is the death card.

"Ugh." Your skin prickles.

Pixie comforts you: "The Dead can be friendly. This means gaining transformation into otherworldly power." Pixie tells you that you are to find a secret séance led by people who practice secret magic.

"To prepare, you must go through an initiation. First you must walk through Pére Lachaise, the cemetery, to face your fears. Then you will be ready to be 'reborn' underground—in the Catacombs. When you find the right secret room, a séance will be awaiting you."

"How exciting, a séance! This is how I can gain fame? Where is it, exactly?"

"Yes, the dead will heighten your powers. You are not told the exact location. The purpose is to learn to feel your way to the secret séance room. Take this map. It will lead you out. Follow each direction like a diligent initiate."

Turn to page 107.

You set out solo and follow all the directions. The cemetery is incredibly spooky. You must recite a walking spell:

> *Spirits of the Dead*
> *Spirits of the Soul*
> *Do not Cower*
> *Help me to gain Power.*

The chanting helps you as you walk through the graves. At the spot marked on the map, you climb down a ladder. You descend into nothingness. You are in the catacombs. "Hello! Anyone around?" Sound echoes into the underground. You light the candle. Surrounding you are walls and walls of skulls. Millions of other bones are piled everywhere.

"Help! Help!" you yell to no one, gulping your fear.

You are lost in a crazy maze. There are so many paths to choose. You walk over bones. You step on crackling remains, trying to feel your way to a séance room. You listen and walk, hoping for the best.

The End

108

"I can do this myself. I am Mata Hari!" You need help but refuse to put your friends in any further danger. You pace the floors of this "Sailing Palace," formulating your plan. Out on the promenade, you marvel at the smokestacks on the ship. You also notice the towering radio poles and wonder if you should send a telegram to Elsbeth and Mr. Astruc with an update. You decide not to.

Clouds gather, and gray skies match your mood. A more seasoned ship traveler told you how a long time ago ships were navigated by the stars. *How did they know when it was cloudy, though?* you wonder.

Lightning crashes and you go inside, passing the lounges full of noteworthy people. You linger in the reading and writing rooms, looking for quiet that might inspire a plan to switch the Dame's cane out.

That night in the dining room, you marvel at the ceiling, a dome filled with night sky and gold stars. Animal and human shapes are painted using the stars, called constellations. Each one has a story and you feel like they are alive. *Perhaps these heavenly beings could help!* You laser-eye the Dame from the back of the room. The show begins on the small stage. You look up: *Heavens, help me!*

Turn to page 115.

You pick the card on the left, the solo journey. The card you reveal is the Devil.

"Yikes!" Fear washes over you.

"The Devil isn't what you think it is. We are going to the salon before you begin your journey."

"Oh wonderful. A salon! I just love getting my hair done."

"Not that kind of salon." Pixie says, and wraps you in black lace, whisking you out to the promenade. The tarantula rides on her hat. This is all very mysterious. You walk through several covered streets, café corners, marveling at Paris with every step. Pixie points out the symbols in the building that stand for a spirit or a religious ideal. She tells you of the artists and thinkers, poets, and spiritualists you are about to meet. None of them is a hairdresser.

Turn to the next page.

"This apartment once belonged to Lady Caithness, a well-known promoter of the invisible arts."

At the door, a regal, female ghost appears before you.

"I am your host, Lady Caithness. Come in," the apparition invites. Her flat is full of symbols, books, and artwork. When you enter the parlor, you meet composers Claude Debussy and Erik Satie, the Dutch painter Mondrian, and the great Irish poet William Butler Yeats. You are drawn to a priest-like character, Joséf Péladan. He has a gown, long beard, and a necklace shaped like a goat's head.

"I once had a carriage driven by goats," you laugh, connecting with him.

Turn to page 112.

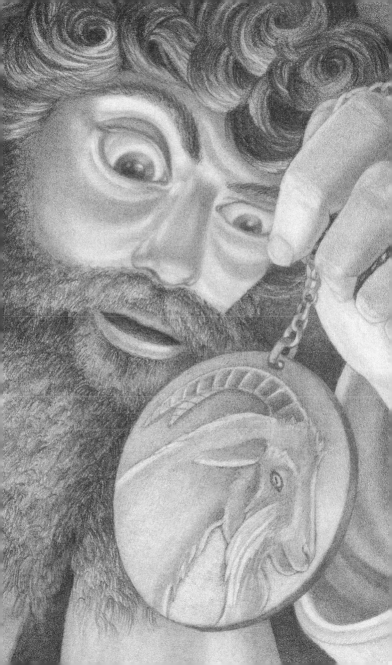

"The symbol of the goat is connected to the cycle of life and death. To rebirth. Of existing in the spaces between old and new," Péladan says, handing you the necklace. "My gift."

With the other guests of the salon, you discuss the role of art and how to make it new. The evening goes on through the night. Everyone is talking about big picture ideas. You plan to collaborate with several of them. You begin working on new, never-before-seen dances. You truly become a part of Parisian life, just as you always dreamed.

The End

"Come with me. I have other friends that can help. We will train you quickly to become a top spy." He brings you to a beach house, with hammocks and a bamboo porch, a room full of tools and drying herbs. He teaches you the plants around the beach jungle, how to collect them and dry them. Then, he makes a concoction and tells you, "Drink this, Mata Hari, it will help you be strong."

You sip it, finding it warm and comforting. Monty keeps talking plants. "The rest will be for the other operatives to show you! But this! This you MUST see." He lifts up the strangest looking flower, a science fiction flower, one with an inviting mouth.

"While you cannot have the monocle, I can leave you with this tip: see this flower? It is a Venus Flytrap. It can attract and eat insects. Be like the flytrap plant. Be like Venus."

Turn to the next page.

114

"Anyway, you'll have to wait here. I have to go on my next mission. The Operatives will arrive to help train and be your guardians."

The room becomes very hazy. The jungle sounds warble. "No, don't leave, Monty!"

"Oh Mata, but I have trained you well. Sort of!" he snickers and trots off.

You are groggy! You can't tell how much time has passed. No one comes. Do you attempt to leave, even though you are so woozy? You can barely make a decision, you are so sedated. You look around as the room fades. The flytrap is inviting, speaking to you. It sounds like it is talking to you. "Come closer," you hear it say. You lean in closer to listen...but you waver, you are under the influence.

"Say that again!" you say, holding it up to your ear. It curls its tendrils at you and flicks its innards. It sucks you in and eats you.

The End

Suddenly, chandeliers are swaying. The ceiling starts to shake: the goat, the fish, the lion, the water-bearer, all start to crumble. You must protect your friends in the dance troupe at any cost. You yell out all their names, yanking the stage curtains to blanket them. But you are not a force against the collapsing room: the zodiac dome caves in.

The End

116

You find the shore not far from the port. It is dusk. You look up to the darkening clouds and spot an enormous balloon. It looks like a potato sailing in the sky, so large it blacks out the setting sun. *Z-42* is painted on its side.

People gather and are afraid. They have heard of these Zeppelins and mutter they are for battling from the air. It's so huge and utterly terrifying to everyone. A hatch opens. You are worried it will produce artillery raining down bullets…

You stare, unsure of your fate.

A glorious, large beam of angelic light shines down, focused on you. It tickles you with a glorious heat and sensation of freedom. The light lifts you up. You levitate.

The End

Traveling with Kali, you state the obvious: "Everything is so gorgeous." Waterfalls and intricate mandalas pepper the landscape, while beautiful mantras are chanted.

"Yes, I created this. And I destroy it. And such is the life of the goddess." She sighs.

"Death is nothing, nor life either, for that matter." You try to comfort her with made-up wisdom.

"Well, we do need one to have the other," Kali says. "Life is not all light. Life can be dark and have demons. Both are necessary. Here, I will show you—which side do you wish to meet?"

"I don't know..."

She grabs and shakes you: "Exactly, you cannot begin to understand it until you live it! Which side?" She cackles as blood pellets fly out of her mouth!

If you choose the powerful destroyer side of Kali, turn to page 120.

Or if you choose Kali Ma, the regenerator and earth mother, turn to page 124.

118

You decide the coded message indicates to go to the Headley Grange. You find a carriage driver and offer him the music box in exchange for a ride.

When you arrive many hours later, you see you are on the grounds of an old farm. You stroll along the fence and barn. Inside you see old uniforms and chains. It must have been an old poorhouse, where orphan children and paupers were housed in exchange for heavy labor.

You approach the stone house that is hundreds of years old. You feel like the ghosts of the workers are following you. You knock using the huge iron ring. You hear dogs barking, so you know someone is home. Someone will have the information you need!

But no, the sounds are approaching from the woods behind you. Little did you know the music box played a song that would save your life by warding off the guard dogs. But you don't have it to play. The pack of wild dogs attack you. Your mission is over.

The End

You figure out that:

JRWRWKHJUDQJH= GOTOTHEGRANGE.

Go to the Grange? The grange listed on the watermark? That is many, many miles away. If you are sure that is the directive, you can catch a horse-and-buggy carriage.

By now you are confused because there are two different messages. You remember that the music box appeared after the commander looked through your trunk. Maybe it's a trap?

If you think the directive is GO TO THE SHORE, turn to page 116.

If you think the directive is GO TO THE GRANGE, turn to page 118.

120

"Well, I do want to destroy the evil and oppression in the world!"

"Ah, great! The Destroyer. Quick, stick out your tongue, Mata Hari, like this."

You stick your tongue out, and it feels silly but liberating. Pink and red rivers flow out, glittering. "RAWR," you mouth, brazen with raw power. Kali lifts her spear out to you.

"My good friend Durga has summoned me to destroy what is known as the 'blood seed.' I have to suck up the bodies that are multiplying out of an endlessly populating demon machine. You're coming, too!"

She snatches you, hooking you on to the spear.

"Well, will removing this evil release Althea from the wrongdoers?" you hope.

"I suppose!" she responds, then shakes all her many hands. They are frightening.

Yet nothing is as frightening as the endless horde you face when you are dropped in a field of multiplying demons. "Tongues out now!" Kali yells. In one fell swoop, she slurps up her swarm of demons. You lap the remnants up, sucking up tiny demons like a vacuum.

While she is triumphant, you get sick. Bloated, you take out your coin and swallow it to try to digest them. But it is too much. Blood balloons in you and you burst. Your head floats off. You die from devouring evil, a hero.

You become the most famous head in the history of saving the world.

The End

122

You put the gloves on and face Commander Page.

"Sorry," you say, "but here is a special kiss from Herr Kramer!" You blow a kiss to him. The wind is too strong. The serum blows back on you, on to your face and into your nostrils. It overwhelms your system. *Everything is an illusion,* you realize. Then you die overloaded with Truth.

The End

You trust the monkey. He leads you safely to a solid stone structure. He has no problem pushing it aside so you can enter the crypt. Inside is incredible darkness: damp floors and walls. Yet you feel a huge grouping of pillows and he indicates you to rest there.

"Um...there doesn't seem to be any sign of Althea."

"You are now a tribute!"

"No, don't you dare leave me," you scream, trying to grab on to the end of the monkey's tail.

"You need this time in quiet darkness. Hahaha." You can hear him laughing his loud monkey laugh. The tombstone closes. And you can't see anything. Maybe someone is coming back, you hope. Then the pillows start expanding, moving closer in. You panic. You suffocate. Darkness leads to the most darkness.

The End

"Ah, my creative side!" Kali says, sweeping you off your feet in a flurry of incense and teleportation. Warmth and protection coat you as you travel. "We are off to Indigo Mountain to meditate!"

Kali is like a jetpack of steam and fire, lifting you, singing in her soothing voice. When you get to the base, she sets you down gently. "Now you must do the journey. You have no choice but to hike. Goodbye, daughter, my eye of the dawn."

"You're leaving me?" you pout. "The mountain is so high!" It also is jiggly, moving nonstop.

Then, a wind blowing from beyond the mountain circles and comforts you: "You can do this," it seems to say. You hike for hours and hours, reminding yourself that there are no shortcuts. Panting, you take out your coin and rub it, hoping for more energy.

When you rub the coin, your forehead buzzes. You feel fuzzy all over. You start breathing in rhythm, singing the songs you learned over and over again. You reach the top. A purple-blue indigo color covers the peak and blends into the sky. It looks like a lake of tranquility.

You sit down to control your breath. Inhale and exhale. The mountain stops moving and shifting. You look down on the earth, grateful for all its glory. "Thanks be to Kali, thanks be to Mother nature." You breathe in the wind from beyond the mountains. You breathe out until you become one with everything.

The End

"I want to take the Dame down," you tell Elsbeth and Mr. Astruc. "I will go to Australia on the SS Orsova."

"Excellent. You will sneak onboard and keep undercover. The Dame must not recognize you! You will have to disguise yourself extremely well. We think you should pose as a man, as a waiter on the ship."

"What else? How will I get home?"

"Once she is apprehended, our colleagues will help transition you home. We will have a contact in Cairns that will help once you dock. Still, we need evidence. She keeps a leather-bound book with all of her notes in a code, and the cipher for the code is in her cane. We need you to take the book and the cane, and replace them with these duplicates," Elsbeth thoroughly explains.

They show you an exact replica of the Dame's book and cane. "Can you handle all that?" Mr. Astruc asks.

"Of course!" you announce, confident.

He hands you a cane and a leather book. Then he explains the papers that will incriminate her, with a hidden message in invisible ink.

"There is a troupe performance scheduled the second night of the trip, just before landing at port. She is arranging a large pick-up of children. And you must act by then."

"Be very careful—your friends could compromise the whole mission if you tell them who you are."

Turn to page 66.

You stand up, trying to act natural, and make your way to the door of your train car. Once you escape the car, you move very fast. You shoot through the space between the cars, on the precipice of danger. The train is approaching a village stop and you must leap before it reaches it. You dive off and roll, aided by your acrobatic skills. You run straight for the woods. Your legs are very strong, and you run fast.

When you look back, you see Ladoux saw you, and he is in hot pursuit. He is small and far away on the hillside, but he's also moving fast.

Go on to the next page.

During your spy training, you learned about the use of camouflage technology in the war. You remember Elsbeth telling you: "Camouflage has evolved in this war, largely driven by women called *camoufleurs*. They practice in parks and dress up like phony rocks and bushes."

You run into the woods where you will have trees and rocks to camouflage in. You quickly find twigs, sticks, a fistful of leaves, and a spot near a stone wall. You camouflage yourself well. You make a peephole. You wait. You think of all the women who were going to work in factories and the fields to feed their families.

You muster all your energy and think about the Greek dancing *maenads* who had claws and magic wands. *Maenads* were women who refused to conform, who could not be captured. *Exactly,* you think. You take out the precious leopard skin pouch you got in Paris, rummage for your hat pin, and tap it to activate the poison. You clutch it in your sweaty hand. You hear Ladoux approaching, and pounce.

"I am Mata Hari! I am a dancing *maenad*. It is I, you traitor, who will have your head!" you scream with all your energy, and you puncture his neck with poison. He crumples. You slay him, wild and victorious.

The End

"Well, the nunnery sounds peaceful," you assume. And it is—at first. You arrive at the nunnery, a towering brick building, so large it tries to touch the heavens. Sister Leonide and Sister Marie give you new clothes to wear, a black tunic with a starched collar and hair cover. "This is called a habit." Immediately, you feel constricted.

"But I like the habits I had: dancing, playing, making a mess, being curious, speaking languages."

"None of that is necessary now. Those habits got you into trouble. So much, we must bathe you in milk to purify you."

"This is so unnecessary! I am not dirty! I just want my clothes and comforts." They deny your requests. You become homesick. Beneath the veneer of purity, the nunnery has rats and cold, damp airless rooms. You write letters to friends and family, day after day, hoping they will rescue you. But the nuns do not send your letters. You get a terrible cough, coughing blood often and becoming frail.

Then you write the nuns, little notes for Marie and Leonide that you will be a good girl. You are desperate, praying to God. "Please help. I need to be free and go live my life," you plead. You gasp for each breath.

You write and write and cough…into oblivion.

The End

The next day, you choose Scarlet and Cleo to help. Bella is too fast and messy, Ruth doesn't pay attention, Anna is too innocent. "Psst! Scarlet, Anna, Bella…" you whisper as you approach their door. "It's me, Margaretha, let me in."

They pull you quickly into their room and you explain everything, jaws dropping. Scarlet agrees to alter the performance, bringing the Dame onstage when it is time to collect an audience member. Cleo will not be performing, so she will duck under the Dame's table and replace the cane. You will be the waiter that slips the new cane to her somehow.

The show begins. Scarlet is onstage, flapping her skirts, with clanging bells on her shoes, rings on her fingers, and begonias in her hair. Everyone is transfixed. During the part where the dancer must find a friend to journey with them, the Dame is pulled onstage, surprised. Leaving her cane behind, Cleo finds the one you slipped under the table. She switches it while the Dame's back is turned toward the audience.

But the Dame has eyes in the back of her head! She whips around and recognizes you. Lunging, she stumbles without her cane. The whole troupe starts grabbing ropes from the nautical decorations. Encircling her, she is knotted up. Now she will know what it's like to be kidnapped! When the steamship arrives at the port in Cairns, the authorities are waiting.

The End

130

You feel your way down the dark hallway, looking for a way out. You see a sign and push open a door beneath it. You drop down into a dingy cavern. You hear the sound of a rushing river overhead. The door shuts behind you before you can turn around. You hope: *maybe this will lead to the train.* Or the subway—you have heard of the newly invented subway train that moves underground.

You crawl through the dampness. Sludge is everywhere. Just as you begin to feel a sense of direction, you enter a cavern. In the middle you make out a large creature with prey in his mouth. His fiery eyes light up the stars on your costume. He smiles as if he recognizes you. He is multi-colored, made of muscle and claws. The monster drips with muck. A sopping wet, well-appointed soldier hangs limp in his mouth.

"I am the Bahkauv! And I have rescued this brave knight from drowning. We have to get him help!"

"Bahkauv, I know a way behind us, but it's tight!" You hop on the back of him. The beast drills space with its claws. Making room as it moves, it pummels a path to bring you all back to safety. Maybe.

The End

"I politely decline," you tell them. "That Ladoux fellow sounds awful—good luck! Now, I am ready to dance in Paris more!"

They look at you quizzically. Molier raises his eyebrow, "Oh, I can hire you!"

The next day you meet him at what appears to be a large circus tent. Inside you see the jugglers, acrobats, monkeys, and clowns rehearsing. *Great! I must be the special guest star.* "Welcome to your new job, Mata," he says, gesturing you to the horse stables. "You will be riding horses. That means you must clean the stalls," he informs you, handing you straw and a bucket.

You have no choice but to spend your days cleaning slop, only to be riding in circles and circles in the circus.

The End

You return through the jungle, reaching a set of stairs that seems to rise endlessly into the sky. You assume they lead to another temple.

Halfway up, you run out of breath, even though you are in such great shape. Near the top, wafts of purple incense smoke surround you. The smoke is so thick, it intoxicates and chokes you. You become dizzy. Very dizzy. The incense totally envelops you, smothering you. You have no control and lose your balance. You do not know whether you are falling to death, only to be reincarnated, or being lifted toward the heavens, only to be reincarnated.

The End

The Story of Mata Hari

Margaretha Zelle was born on August 7, 1876, in the Netherlands. She had three younger brothers and was very close with her father. Mata and her father both loved unusual things, and when she was six years old he gave her a goat-drawn cart to take to school, which her classmates thought was spectacular.

Margaretha's father ran a hat-making business that became very successful and popular when she was a child, and the family moved to a large house. Margaretha attended an exclusive boarding school where she learned etiquette, languages, and performing arts. When Margaretha was 19, she married a Dutch Army soldier and moved to the Indonesian island of Bali.

On Bali, Margaretha and her husband, Rudolph MacLeod, had two children. Life was difficult and strange on the island, and Margaretha's young son died in a tragic poisoning. Margaretha fled home to Holland. From there, she made a plan.

Margaretha moved to Paris and involved herself in the art world during an exciting time. She invented a stage persona, Lady MacLeod, and performed dances she had learned while she lived in Bali. Invitations poured in for her popular stage show.

She was invited to dance in the Library of Oriental Art in the Museum Guimet. The owner, a man named Monsieur Guimet, suggested she dance under the name Mata Hari, which means Eye of the Dawn in Malay, the language spoken in Bali. This is the moment that her life as Mata Hari began.

Mata Hari began dancing across Europe on stages in Italy, France, Paris, and Germany. Her dances were mysterious and exciting. Crowds came to see her and famous musicians, composers, and dance choreographers traveled to work with her. She developed friendships with famous and powerful people.

When World War I began in Europe, both German and French Army Intelligence hoped to convince Mata Hari to use her skills for languages and her talents to draw secrets out of the people she met during her travels, secrets that could win the war.